HouseGuest

Episode Seven
ORPHAN DREAMER SAGA
A Novelette: Asher Bushcroft

J. NELL BROWN

Orphan Dreamer Saga: Episode Seven
The Houseguest: A Novelette

Published by J. Nell Brown, LLC and Rogue Reads, LLC

For ordering information, contact the publisher via the author's website, www.JNellBrown.com.

Printed in the United States of America.

Second Edition, 2018

Cover by: www.whiterabbitgraphix.com and FrinaArt

ROGUE READS
LLC

BOOKS BY
J. Nell Brown

NONFICTION

Shhh, My Father Is Speaking, and I Am Listening: A Bible Study on Hearing God's Voice

Blood Moon—God's Warning: Why Knowledge of Jewish Feasts Is Essential to Understand the Blood Moons of 2014 and 2015

FICTION

Orphan Dreamer Saga
Orphan Dreamer and the Missing Arrowhead

Orphan Dreamer and the Glass Tattoo

She Laughs Last

Orphan Tree: Rooted in Eternal Love

Collector's First Edition Paperback
The Omega Journey: Blood Moons Whisper

COMING SOON

A Generation of Lighted Evergreens

Orphan Falls: Wild and Free

House Guest

Orphan Star: The Mark

Little Peach Lies

Orphan's Seed

If Love's a Fish

Orphan's Horizon

Orphan's End

1

IMMORTALS —TIME WITHOUT END

I'M IN A COLD CAVE, which is rather ironic because I'm in hell.

Tsk. Tsk. Don't pity me. After the moon drips with blood, I will come for you. Until then, I'm here at my summer residence, prepping for our meeting—Armageddon, the day I scrub Earth clean of its invaders.

You.

My most treasured possession sits beside me while humans squint, then peek through the optics of a telescope only to ask, "Is there an intelligent life form in outer space?" I laugh. Only a nitwit and self-centered creature would look into a telescope and ask such a stupid question.

If a creature requires a telescope to see me, they are working at a disadvantage.

I see you.

Here's looking at you, kid. No optics. No lens. No convex shiny mirrors. No telescope. And now it's my turn to ask, "Does any intelligent life exist on Earth?"

I already know the answer: No, not yet. But very soon. I look down past Earth's atmosphere. The moon is full. Bright. White. One day it will darken to blood red at the right time. Then, we will come back, and there will only be enough room for one species—mine.

"Welcome home, Nomed," I say to myself, eager for the day when Aglaope whispers these three words into my ear as we stand side by side on the sugary-white beaches of Key West, Florida, or the snow-packed ridges of Mount Everest. I love the cold. It suits me.

"You're in good practice." Aglaope smiles at me.

"I'm ready. No. *We're* ready to return home, Agla." I gaze into the distance. Cloaked in secrecy, my winter home approaches Earth. Ah, when a plan comes together!

We call our Trojan horse Wormwood. Larger than the sun, the invisible planet hides in the shadows of Earth's universe, deep in a wormhole that no human has dared to explore. Besides, the inky black entrance into that wormhole appears as a tiny speck through Earth's most powerful telescopes. My warriors train day and night in preparation for our day of reckoning—the day we invade Earth and take it back, making the planet great once again.

"When they see Wormwood, it will be too late, Agla."

"And that's why you're his general, Nomed. Cunning. Ruthless. Decisive." Her left eye scarred shut, Aglaope gazes into my left eye. "Could a human fight your warriors and win?"

"Of course."

"But you promised me!" She pulls away from my embrace. "You promised that all would be well. That I would be safe."

"They could win if they knew how to fight us. But they don't know how to fight us, and their bullets, nuclear warheads, aircraft carriers, and submarines will be useless in this fight. They will kill themselves. But not us. Never fear. Humans couldn't figure out how to give life if they tried. How long have they played around in the most prestigious laboratories, yet not cured cancer?"

"This weapon . . ." Aglaope reaches for my hand. "What is it?"

"I hold this secret closer to my bosom than I have held you."

"Nomed, tell me," she whines.

"No! It's for your protection, my love. Do not ask me again."

"The reconnaissance team left an hour ago. Why?" She's a sneaky interrogator. I smile. Use her skills to defeat the humans.

"Small. Spindly. Weak man and woman." I spit. Acid eats away at the stone floor of our cave. "Any threat to our victory will be destroyed. You have suffered because of them, now they will suffer because of you, Agla."

"My defender." She blushes. "Nomed, purge the humans immediately—don't wait. I fear in time they will gain strength. Tell our leader, okay?"

"No. Let them do their part, slaughtering their neighbor—man, woman, and child—for every reason under the sun. They love death. Then, death they shall have. Fools they are, eliminating their own warriors."

"But you'll save the animals? The snake? The shark? The grizzly?"

"Yes, my love. We will protect Earth's animals. They are the civilized species on Earth."

"Have this man and woman seen us? Do they know we are coming?"

"Coming—no. Exist—they call us aliens. Little green men with big black eyes. I've seen the artistic renderings." I laugh, again.

"Aliens? Little green men?" Aglaope laughs too, covering her twisted lips. She used to be beautiful.

"They call us extraterrestrials . . . as though we're side actors in their play."

"Silly, they are."

"They do not deserve life, and I intend to put Earth out of its misery." I squeeze Aglaope's hand.

"Then, death you shall gift—but remember, protect our people. Promise me, Nomed."

"Aglaope." I place my hand across my heart and stand at attention. "As general of our powerful army, I promise this to you: on that day of reckoning—Earth's Armageddon—not one man or woman will spill the innocent blood of our warriors, but I will flood Earth's rivers, lakes, and oceans with their blood, human blood. The vultures, sea monsters, and hyenas will feast for days. And you and I . . . we will celebrate and then make you well again."

"We will celebrate. Earth will be cleansed. Livable once more. Purge the humans from our home soon, Nomed. I want to be well."

"Agla, I am a powerful creature, but do I decide when Earth moves in between the sun and the moon?"

A tear slips from her right eye as she whispers, "No, and that's what I'm afraid of. He does." Her emphasis fell on 'he'.

"Tell me your fears, my love. I will crush them." I ball my hands into fists. My claws dig into my skin. Green slime oozes from my body. I would bleed dry for Aglaope.

"I am afraid. You've discounted the One who flung the moon, the stars, and the sun into space."

"No! They have discounted the One."

"Even still," her voice drops. "He may fight for them— man and woman. If He fights for them, they will win this war."

"Why would He? They care nothing for Him. They distort everything He creates."

Thump, scrape, thump, scrape—the sound of metal slapping and then dragging along a granite floor pounds in my ears. The master is approaching.

I crouch low. "Hide, Aglaope."

She slinks around the corner of the small cave, down the usual passage of a set of narrow stone steps before disappearing into a smoky haze. My body aches for her, but she's gone. Only the stench of sulfur remains, my constant reminder of my failure—my failure to Aglaope.

"No-o-o-med . . . No-o-o-med, where are you?" My master's voice haunts my ears, chatters my teeth.

"Here, my lord." I shift my weight, kneel, then lie prostrate.

My master's iridescent, snakelike form slithers at lightning speed through the underworld, vibrating the stagnant, thick air. Black smoke belches from a cauldron of burning sulfur while screams of lost souls reverberate in the background. Eerie dissonant tones erupt from a contraption that resembles a splintered pipe organ as my master charges toward me. "Bow before me."

I propel my reptilian body atop the black granite floor, careful to remain prostrate before my master. I rotate my scaly neck and peek at Lucifer. When he blinks, black-green scales flicker over his neon-green eyes. His razor-toothed maw widens. Yellowed, jagged teeth reveal his pleasure. *Oh, to be worshiped!* "Stand."

I rise like a king cobra.

"Go to the viewing room." Lucifer struts past me.

I jump up and run on iridescent green-black webbed feet, overlaid with fingerlike claws. "A plan, my lord?"

"No. War!" Lucifer marches deeper into the cavern.

"Our forces are fatigued."

"That's your fault. Not mine." Something burns in his wake. "Elohim's planning His final act."

"The end," I whisper, scampering behind my master.

A towering wall of luminescent green gel wobbles before us—the portal to the viewing room where images of the future are revealed.

"The viewing room's images haven't been reliable in the past," I say.

"We've identified Elohim's agents before," my master says.

I grimace as I stare at the gelatin wall. Sensing my fear, it shoots biting ice shards into my leathery scales. They stab my flesh like a thousand fragments of glass. I clench my teeth, enduring the pain. "Are we to be banished?"

"Questions won't stop Elohim, only actions."

"C-c-can we stop Him?"

"Stop His agents. That's always been the way." Lucifer grins wide, revealing pearlescent white fangs. Sometimes my master appears dashing, but other times . . .

Lucifer slips his claws through the wall of green gel. Reluctantly, I follow. Haunting voices from the future mix with screeches belonging to readers who channel the future. A fuzzy image plays on a stony wall in the dark room—a séance.

"Out!" The petrol station worker grabs twelve-year-old Joseph by his ripped T-shirt and throws him across the room. His body slams into a brick wall. Dazed, the boy scrambles to get on his feet and run, but the man jumps on him again and starts kicking him repeatedly in the gut.

"Please! Please!" He cries between labored breaths. "I'll leave. Just let me get up."

"Don't come back." The man stops kicking. "Next time, I'll douse you with petrol and set you on fire."

"Yes, sir. I . . . promise . . ." There's no breath left for words, so Joseph crawls from the warm room into a cold Manchester evening. The icy wind barrels past his threadbare clothes and jolts a shiver up his body. He grips the window ledge, pulls himself to his feet, and stumbles along until he finds his new home behind a dumpster. If the Irish-Scots boy could remember how Mama Kelly had prayed, he would beg to fall asleep and never wake up. Yahweh is the name she'd prayed to. Joseph may not know the

name, but he hopes her God doesn't hate him as much as most adults do.

"Elohim's agent is a twelve-year-old homeless boy." I burst into laughter. "He won't survive until morning."

"You fool. He's not just any twelve-year-old. That's Cillian Joseph Finn."

I stare at the ground.

"David killed Goliath—a shepherd boy killed a giant with a stone and a sling."

"That was an anomaly."

"You judge nothing." Lucifer strolls to my side. "Don't let another anomaly occur."

"Yes, my lord. Should I rouse the force?"

"Not yet. The readers say there's another agent."

I gaze back at the stony wall. Echoes of screams deliver their message.

A twelve-year-old girl named Rose stands at the edge of the creek, watching a water moccasin slither through the water. She slides off her shoes and socks, then dips her right toe into the cold water. Would the snake's bite hurt? Would death come quickly? The kids at school hate her. They say she's too smart or too dumb. Then what is she?

Alone.

She steps into the water and approaches the snake. It stops, turns, and waits. What about Daddy? He's sick. Mom? She'd miss her. Her reflexes ignore the warning growing in her mind. She strides toward her choice of death.

"Stop!" Her teacher calls from the field behind her, but the determined child sloshes through the stream closer to the snake. Her foot slides over a smooth rock hidden in the creek bed. Losing her balance, she crashes into the pond. The snake floats inches from her head and rises above the water's surface, ready to strike.

Someone splashes into the water beside Rose's shoulder. Hands grip her arms, pulling her from the creek. "What on earth are you doing?"

Rose's shoulders start shaking. "I . . . I'm sorry, Ms. Jenkins. I . . . I'm so sad."

"What are you saying?"

The little girl wags her head, then falls into her teacher's embrace.

"You listen to me and listen real good. Before you were born, Yahweh tucked away great plans for you. Your kindred friend will come. Just you wait and see."

"Yes, ma'am." Rose smiles.

I roll my torso erect and laugh. "She's a girl, and a stupid one at that. What twelve-year-old entertains Death and wins?"

"Her mother did."

"I forgot, my lord." I bow low.

"See that Death wins this time."

"Kill her?"

Lucifer smiles. "You wanted a promotion—more time on Earth. Earn it."

"You're generous, master."

"Don't forget it."

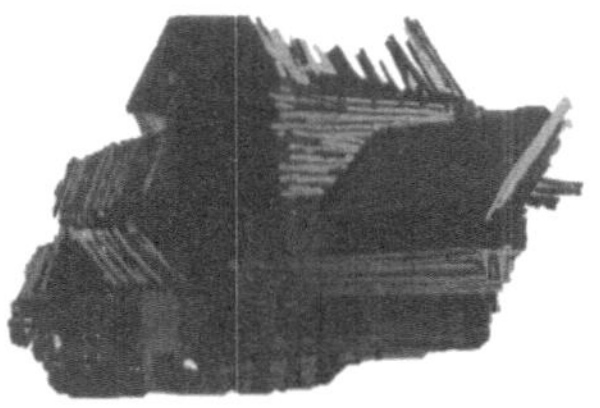

2

"WERE YOU PAYING ATTENTION BACK in the viewing room?" My master paces a dark hall that's crawling with maggots. Today, the black granite rocks are overrun with molten lava and protrude inward, suffocating me and preventing me from expressing my objections.

"I . . . I have my own opinions." I slink back until the fiery wall stops my retreat. I smell burning flesh—my flesh. Sweat pours down my face. I dare not move an inch.

My master stops pacing, turns, and crawls close. Erecting his body, his breath blows hot across my skin, scalding my face. "Since when did your opinions matter?"

"Never."

"Speak."

"I've served you faithfully, but why kill the homeless Irish boy? He's a nobody." I think of my son—half mortal, half immortal, a Nephilim.

"Learn his name. Joseph! Can you remember that?"

"Of course, my lord, but he's not a young prophet like the other child—the one with the long blonde hair, arctic-blue eyes, and blushed cheeks." I snap my fingers and bow my head, hoping the name comes back to my memory . . . and that my slyly deceptive description of the brown-skinned girl pleases my lord. My master digs his claw across my face, opening a wound.

"R-r-rose." I spit out the word. "A perfect name for a beautiful girl."

"Daniela Rose Cavanaugh. And stop drooling."

But how could I? Long blonde hair, arctic-blue eyes, and blushed cheeks. Is this truly the description of my victim—Rose? I want her to look like I imagine, a Nordic angel. But my master shatters my illusion with a name—Daniela Rose Cavanagh.

Besides, demons can't be expected to get everything right. Blonde hair or brown. Blue eyes versus black. Lily pale skin versus brown. Who cares? I prefer to chase a Swedish bombshell. So, I will.

My master stops cutting. "Rose is more powerful, but she's transferring her power to the little boy."

"How?"

"Prayer, you fool. It's what Elohim's agents do."

"Why?"

"That's why I'm sending you. Go find out, and then get rid of her and the little Irish boy."

"And I'll get a promotion?"

Lucifer smirks, amused at my selfishness. "So quickly your concern for the boy wanes."

"But Death lives in Germany, and it's not fair that I'm stuck here with the ordinary demons."

"It seems Elohim means to end our fun sooner rather than later."

"How can you tell?"

"I prowled His dimension—the place where time does not exist. He commanded Legna, that groveling, obedient warrior, to go into the land of the mortals. To Babylon."

"When?"

"575 BCE."

"That was ages ago."

"Even so. Legna will be disguised, but you must find him. Stop him." Balls of fire fly from Lucifer's maw and pelt the ground around my feet. I scrabble left and then right, struggling to dodge my master's fiery spittle. "Elohim means to cast us into the fiery pit for eternity."

My rotting teeth rattle, and I scratch the granite floor with my black ice-pick claws. "And the humans will keep our home—Earth?"

"Not without a fight. The Lord of the Flies still prepares on Venus—in case you fail. Wormwood is almost complete." Lucifer sheds his iridescent scales. They clatter to the floor like hail pummeling glass. Blood-red claws erupt from his tail as legs protrude from his slithering form. A lion's mane borders his crimson eyes, set in a gargoyle-like face.

I stumble backward. After falling to the ground, I lie prostrate.

"I prodded Nebuchadnezzar to destroy Judah and enslave Ezekiel, the prophet," Lucifer says. "What went wrong?"

"Who knows?"

"Slavery should have made them curse Elohim. But Ezekiel scampered around Babylon, cradling armfuls of scrolls and looking ridiculous."

"I can make Elohim's agents stop scampering. The promotion?"

"Of course I'll promote you in the ranks. Would I ever lie to you?"

If you'd been honest about the real estate down here, I wouldn't have participated in your little rebellion up there. "No, my lord."

"Go discover His plans." My master sheds his dashing, handsome face. He grins, his ugly maw filled with rotten fangs. "Possess any willing human. Destroy Elohim's prophet. Ezekiel's presence spells the end—the end of my time." Fire spews from the old dragon's mouth and lands on my side. "Find Asher. You'll be Asher's houseguest until Rose and Joseph are dead. Be gone."

I roll away and retch a hellish scream. I clutch my side and quickly pull my hand away. A sticky mixture of scalded, deep green-black scales cling to my claws.

"Stop screaming! Stop that prophet and his future hirelings. Earth belongs to me!" Lucifer stamps his foot into the ground.

The underworld shakes.

Humans call it an earthquake.

"Asher. Asher. Asher," I repeat the name, hoping not to forget my ticket to a promotion as I scurry toward the tunnel leading out of the underworld. "I'm getting a promotion," I sing and dash up the chute's walls. The scent of fresh earth fills my nose. My claws scratch boulders as I pick up speed and transform into something beautiful. I smile, leaving the stench of sulfur behind. In the mortal realm, my confidence strengthens.

They are ignorant of my presence and assignment. Ignorance was never more blissful.

3

Cosmic Half-Revolution

MY NAME'S NOMED, AND I'M a houseguest.

I don't possess a surname, because my ancestry is complicated. But my host, Asher Bushcroft, is a simple boy. He invited me to be his houseguest, or maybe I invited myself. Details don't matter. He's obedient to those he fears, so he'll tell our story.

I can be vulnerable, so I'll share a secret. I'm obsessed with two children: Rose Cavanaugh, an American, and Joseph Finn, an Irish-Scot. They're not related, at least not yet. Just the fact they possess surnames shows they're simple, like Asher.

Don't think me petty.

I'm not obsessed with Rose and Joseph for simple reasons. Neither is popular at school, nor rich. Quite the opposite. But my master believes their futures will be complicated and powerful and could potentially wreak havoc on my world. We won't talk about my master, because I'm on vacation from my hellish job to talk to you. But I'll share my master's final instructions: *Murder Rose and Joseph before they accomplish the mission.*

Death and I are great friends, so I intend to have fun while carrying out my mission. But I needed help. A host. So I found Asher. He obliged, in exchange for a favor. I wanted to be Rose's or Joseph's houseguest, but some meddling human prayed for them, protecting them from my visit. So Legna, Yahweh's groveling servant, blocked my visitation. Parents . . . why do they pray for their children?

I'll introduce you to Legna in another tale.

There's no need to tell the kids' stories; someone else can do that. That is, if they survive my assignment. But if they survive, I don't. Nor does my family. I grind my teeth just thinking about both of them.

A warning: They won't survive my schemes, because I need a promotion. A promotion means better assignments, and I'm dying to live in America permanently—even though my friend Death loves Germany, especially the camps. We meet up in Paris for vacation.

We have Asher. He's human, so earthlings acknowledge Asher's existence. But they deny mine. That's okay. There's no battle when the victim doesn't know he has an enemy. And that makes me smile . . . widely.

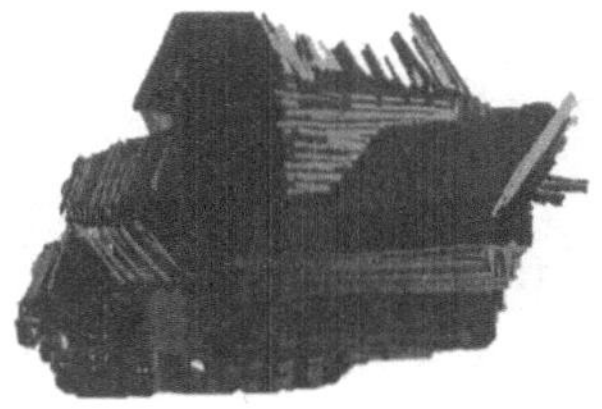

4

YESTERDAY, A VILLAIN WAS BORN.

I, Asher Valerian Bushcroft, am that villain, but 1941 wasn't my birth year.

My birthday occurred twelve years ago when my mother, Ruth Bushcroft, pushed me from between her thighs onto white cotton sheets. My father, Reuben, was probably sitting by a window, reading a newspaper.

I'm riding in the backseat of my parents' 1941 Mercedes Benz. My mother grips the steering wheel at the nine o'clock and three o'clock positions as she drives five miles

under the speed limit on the highway. We're on our way to
Sing Sing Prison in Ossining, New York.

I stare at my mother as she glances at me in the mirror. She's nervous. I can sense the emotion by the way she
taps the steering wheel with her red-lacquered nails. She
averts her eyes toward Father. He sits in the passenger seat,
reading his newspaper. "We're doing the right thing by the
boy?" she asks quietly.

Father grunts. I don't know if that means yes or no.

My sister, Natalia, isn't here.

She's dead. Died at 1:23 p.m. One fine summer morning
at the age of sixteen.

I was at the scene. I push myself up in my seat to look
in the rearview mirror. Nothing's changed. I'm still ugly.
Pink dots must have rained down on my face while I was
sleeping and stuck like glue. My ears could be mistaken for
our neighbor's basset hound's. Natalia was tall and grace-
ful, with flawless skin. She loved to dance and even tried to
teach me, but I was hopelessly clumsy.

Nomed makes me roll my eyes, a facial expression I
could control yesterday morning, but not anymore. I focus
on the Star of David dangling from the rearview mirror.

A few minutes ago, Adolf Hitler declared war on the
United States of America, or maybe it was the other way
around. I remember the day, about a year ago, when we left
our house in Berlin, Germany.

Patience.

Let me share my memories.

5

IT WAS A COLD, GRAY morning, and the weather matched my mood.

Draped around our pine tree, white Christmas lights sparkled. Another example of my father's failing assimilation into Germany's secular culture. The sweet, earthy scent of pine mixed with cinnamon sticks—my sister's favorite house scent—permeated the two-bedroom apartment.

I found the odor noxious.

Father raced from our dresser drawers back to our suitcases, throwing clothes and shoes into my sister's and my cases. His black knee-high boots thudded along the ash wood floor. Sweat poured down his temples, and he unbuttoned the jacket of his ink-black SS uniform, revealing a soaked undershirt.

"Father, where are we going?" I asked.

"Away."

"Should I tell Natalia?"

"No. She'll find out, Vale." When my father was anxious, he called me a shortened version of my middle name—Valerian. I hated the name. He forced a smile across his face and winked. "Let her see the world as she wishes . . . daffodils, music, and butterflies. He placed his fingers on my shoulders, and his manicured hands felt like lead weights. "We'll celebrate your twelfth birthday in America, okay?"

I nodded, liking the idea of traveling; escaping would be even better.

High heels tapped across the floors as Mother entered my bedroom. "Why is your uniform unbuttoned, Reuben? The ball is tonight." Reuben was my father's real name, but Germans who weren't Jewish called him Ryland. My mother sucked another drag from her long brown cigarette as she tapped her crimson-red painted nails on the doorframe. "Listen to me."

My father continued his frantic pace, yanking open the closet door and grabbing my favorite sweater. "If you'd help, I wouldn't have to run around like a baboon in heat."

"I told you. I won't leave Germany." My mother crossed her arms, and my sister walked into our bedroom. "What's going on?" My parents ignored her.

"Stupid woman. I should grant your wish and only take the children." My father glanced at my sister and me. His expression registered panic and fear. "But they need their mother."

"Reuben, you've got a fine job—"

"Is that what you call it? A fine job?"

"You've never wanted me to be happy. I finally have a social life that is the envy of German socialites."

"Cracked egg. That's what you are."

My mother marched toward my father and slapped him across the face. "Don't disrespect me in front of the children!" Her slaps had become more frequent, but my father never hit back.

"I'm wrong." Father's face paled. "You're selfish and evil."

Hatred pulsed between the two. Trembling, I backed up until the window stopped my retreat. I wished I had never turned around. But I did. I looked out of our second-story window. Two men dressed like my father pounded on a door across the street.

A man with rumpled nightclothes opened the door.

The uniformed men grabbed him.

Soldiers dressed in gray barreled into the house, dragging out a little girl and a woman in nightdresses. I yanked the curtains shut, blocking out whatever was going on outside. "F-f-father." I glanced at my father's spit-polished, black leather boots and shivered. "Would you kidnap Mister Gutenberg's family—our neighbors?"

"Don't worry, son." He embraced me. "I . . . I'm not like them."

"What are you like, Father?"

"I'm a good father." His voice broke. "I've protected my family. Done the best I could."

"I love you, Papa, and one day, I'll be like you." I embraced him, needing to feel safe.

"Do you know what your father does?" Mother sneered.

"Shut up, woman!" My father raised his hand, preparing to strike her. It would have been the first time he'd slapped her—and in my book, she deserved it, constantly picking on Natalia and humiliating Father. He stepped back and retracted his hand.

"Stop arguing," Natalia begged, then placed her violin inside its case. I dragged my suitcase to the front door. "I'm glad we're leaving Germany. This place scares me."

My mother ran her fingers across a gold necklace dangling from her neck—her favorite, given to her before Grandmother died five years ago. A pendant hung from the chain—a circle surrounding a six-pointed star. Mother called the symbol the Star of David, but Father said it was evil and called it the Seal of Solomon. "Take that pendant off." His voice was controlled, but I could tell he wanted to scream. Neck veins protruded and his face turned a deep crimson.

"Natalia's wearing hers." No different than a tattletale, my mother pointed toward the dainty gold chain hanging around my sister's neck. Father ripped the necklace from Natalia. She whimpered, and I stepped forward, ready to fight my father.

"Mother gave it to me." My mother lifted her chin. "It's a family heirloom."

"More like a noose. Are you willing to die for it?" All was quiet, except for my father's heavy breathing. He was angry, and my mother was thinking for a change. She twirled on her pink pumps and strode from the room.

Who knew what the real story was behind that pendant. Occasionally, both of my parents had been known to embellish facts. Quietly, I dressed, and we followed Father down dimly lit alleys to a waiting car.

That night, we escaped Germany on an evening train. Mother stopped fussing when Natalia pulled her violin from its case. "Natalia, where did you get that? That's a Stradivarius."

My sister clutched the instrument to her chest. "The Gutenbergs. Their son . . . he gave it to me yesterday morning."

"Why?"

"He said the teacher at school placed his family's name on a list."

Something seemed to click in Mother's head, but she didn't speak of her newfound knowledge. Instead she kept her mouth shut, which became a family habit. Silence ruled.

Then, one gloomy day nearly a year later—December 11, 1941—madman Adolf Hitler declared war on the United States of America.

On that day, Father stopped reading his newspaper, and the mute spoke for the first time in a long time. "The condemned Gutenberg's Stradivarius spared our lives. Let's make the best of it."

My sister played a sweet tune on the Stradivarius, and father joined the American military. He went back to Germany and kicked Hitler butt.

Adolf is why I ended up in America—and why I became a villain.

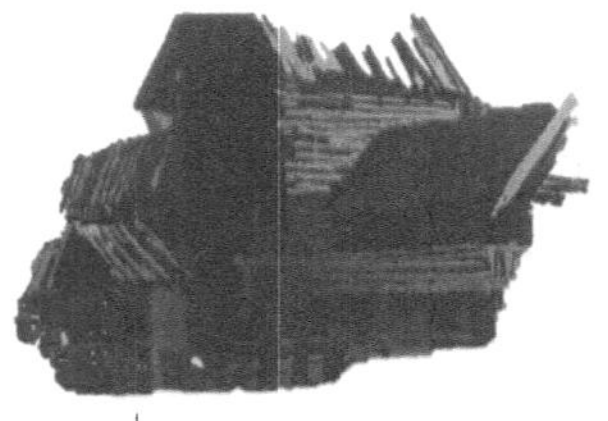

6

HOW DID I BECOME A villain?

Four days ago, on the last day of school before summer break, Annaliese—the prettiest girl in school—told me I'm too short and my muscles too flabby to have the privilege of writing her love notes. I voiced my concern about her preference for a seventeen-year-old boy over me. We're only twelve. Maybe I shouldn't have liked girls at twelve, but I liked Annaliese.

Dutifully, Annaliese's friends explained that I wasn't tall, cute, or WASPy enough for their fair-haired, East Hampton friend.

I waited until the house was quiet to share the humiliating news with my sister. After watching my parents fall asleep in their respective recliners, I snuck into Natalia's bedroom. She sat on the edge of her bed with her back to the door, running a brush through her curls. Her hair draped over her shoulders.

I stopped at the doorway, hung my head, and cried.

Natalia laid her brush on her bed and turned. "What's wrong?"

"It's Annaliese."

Without saying a word, she walked across the room, shut the door behind me, and dropped the needle onto an old vinyl record. Soft bass vibrations mixed with a soulful piano played a languid tune. "Come here, Asher."

I stumbled into her arms. She talked to me the way I wished Annaliese would. But I had Natalia, and for that moment, I was grateful. Unusual for me, I must have fallen asleep on her bed, because the next day I awoke to find my sister sleeping on the floor. "Natalia . . ." I shook her shoulders until she stirred.

She moaned and rolled over.

"Natalia, good morning. Wake up."

She stretched and yawned. "What time is it?"

"I don't know, but it's bright outside. Let's play chess on the front porch."

She stood, and as she walked, her wrinkled pink-and-white nightgown swayed around her ankles. I waited and gave her a few minutes of privacy, then joined her in the bathroom.

After we brushed our teeth, I went to my bedroom and flung a white cotton shirt around my shoulders. I returned to my sister's room, where she helped me roll the cuffs. She had ironed the shirt herself the day before. Mother hated to iron, Father never looked up from his paper, and Natalia didn't trust me with anything hot. A year ago, I had burned a hole in her favorite blouse, and she hadn't forgotten.

Natalia covered her palms in Brylcreem and stroked my head, rubbing the mineral oil and beeswax into my hair, leaving a wet look to my unruly henna curls. "Don't worry about Annaliese. I love you."

"Like the girl in Mother's book?"

"What book?"

"The one with the muscled man on the front. The one she always has her nose buried in."

"You didn't read that, did you?"

"Did you?"

"You shouldn't have." Natalia turned up my collar. "There. Now you're just as cool as the boy Annaliese crushes on."

"If cool means looking like I'm in first grade instead of seventh."

"You didn't decide your height."

"Who did?"

"Adonai."

"Well, then He and I have a problem, Miss Giraffe."

"Adonai isn't your enemy. You'll figure that out soon enough." Natalia giggled, revealing a row of metal braces.

"We'll make an agreement—He stays over there, and I stay over here."

She shook her head, showing her disapproval.

I followed Natalia to the living room of our East Hampton house. It was the usual scene: Father sat in his recliner, reading the paper; Mother rolled the dials on the old radio with her pinky finger and thumb. A long brown cigarette dangled between her forefinger and middle finger. She plopped into her recliner and laughed frequently as actors ran through their lines.

My sister and I loved to play chess. If my parents had allowed it, we'd have played from the time we woke up until we fell asleep. But there also were chores that needed to be done. Everyone else in our neighborhood hired help, but my mother told our neighbors she didn't need a house-keeper because her house was naturally spotless. She really meant that the house was spotless from the efforts of her natural-born children, but who needed the details?

"Mother, what do you want for breakfast?" Natalia stood beside Mother's recliner.

"Pancakes, bacon, and milk." No *good morning* or *how are you.* "Make sure the bacon is crispy. Yesterday, it was floppier than a wilted flower."

A Jewish mother eating bacon was odd. Besides, what did Mother know about flowers? She never went outside, unless she wanted to gossip with Mabel, our nosy neighbor. According to my mother and Mabel, their marriages, opinions, and disciplinary styles were the gold standard for everyone else. I wanted to roll my eyes at the thought of bacon and flowers, but today I was in control of my actions, so I didn't.

After receiving Mother's daily cooking criticisms, Natalia disappeared into the kitchen.

My sister was smart—a genius—too smart to be taking orders like a waitress in a diner. Her efforts made me want to try harder so I could become rich and one day hire her a maid.

She wanted to attend Julliard on a violin scholarship. The violin she'd played in front of the admission committee was that same Stradivarius she'd gotten from our Jewish neighbors back in Germany. Natalia had told me the Gutenbergs lost their connections. They were rich, so I didn't understand why they gave it to her for safekeeping. According to my father, the Gutenbergs were still in Germany, suffering, while Natalia was in New York making music.

In Natalia's defense, when we left Germany one year ago, she'd told me she couldn't stop crying the day she took the violin from their thirteen-year-old son. The next night, before we left, the Gutenberg family was shipped to some sort of camp for Jewish people. Natalia hadn't explained more than that. She'd seemed to know more, but when I'd asked questions, she kept her mouth shut.

After our chores and lunch, Natalia and I played chess on the porch from noon until dinnertime.

"Checkmate," she said.

"Again?"

"Seems like it." Natalia looked at her watch, and then I looked at mine. She jumped up. "I'm late."

"For what?"

"It's past six o'clock." She bolted into the kitchen and started opening cabinets, removing pots and pans.

"I'll help," I say.

"You know Mother doesn't like your cooking."

"And I don't like hers."

Natalia shook her head. "You're impossible."

About thirty minutes later, we sat down to eat. None of us uttered a word throughout the meal.

I went upstairs, showered, dressed in my pajamas, and climbed into bed, hoping Natalia would sneak into my bedroom with cookies and milk in hand. The radio still blared downstairs, so she wouldn't dare venture back into the kitchen to steal food, and I was too scared to do it myself.

Lights out. The darkness surrounded me.

I would become used to darkness.

7

A STRANGE NOISE WOKE ME at two in the morning—*thump, scrape, thump, scrape.*

The sound reminded me of an old pirate dragging his wooden leg across the deck of his ship. My brocade curtains were fully open, and the full moon cast an eerie glow across my bedroom's wooden floorboards. The sound came from outside, or so I hoped.

Pulling my covers up to my chin, I slid closer to the foot of the bed and held my breath, waiting. Barely tilting my chin up, I surveyed my bedroom.

Thump, scrape, thump, scrape—the sound grew louder. I squeezed my eyelids shut and plugged my ears with my fingers, but the sound intensified, as though it originated from inside my head.

Disturbed, I unplugged my ears and sat up. The sound amplified again. So it wasn't in my head. Looking out from my east-facing window, I gazed at the lake. Behind the boathouse on the other side of the river, a green mist swirled above the water and then moved to the center of the lake. I laid my hand on my chest, keeping my heart from galloping past my ribs and flesh.

I climbed out of bed, tiptoed to the window, and placed my hand on the windowsill. A cool breeze seeped around the casing, numbing my fingers. I rested my hand on the glass pane. It was warm. Confused, I stepped away from the window.

Something hard hit my back.

I gasped and swung around. My eyes darted from left to right.

No one.

Nothing, except the outline of the footboard of my four-poster bed. I turned back to the window. Two neon-green dots rose from the black lake into the mist, hovered, disappeared, and then reappeared as though someone was signaling in Morse code. My imagination again—I loved reading spy books.

The dots continued their disappearing-reappearing ritual, and then the *scrape-thump* sound silenced.

Quiet, except for the pounding of my heart in my ears.

Eyes?

They must be.

As though they sensed my understanding, the neon eye-like dots moved from the center of the lake and stopped over our boat dock. My heart jackhammered against my ribs.

The green mist swirled beneath the neon eyes and took on a black, dense form—like a body. The eyes stopped at the shoreline, paused, then flew back to the center of the lake and vanished beneath the black surface. Moonlight illuminated the cracked ice and a ripple of water as the mist took form, spread outward, and then disappeared.

I backed away from the window, my eyes fixed on the lake. Reaching behind me, I grabbed my sheets and crawled back into bed. This time, I pulled the blanket and sheets over my head.

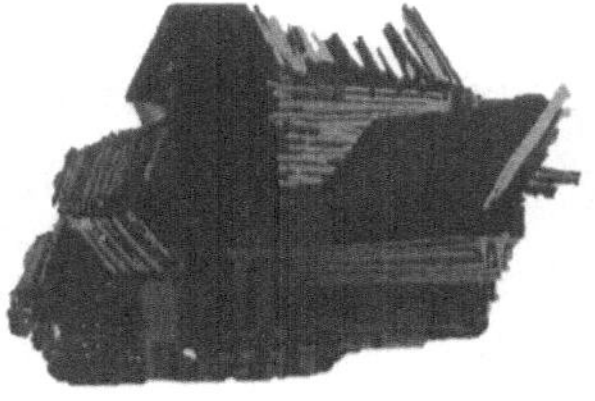

8

"ASHER." A SWEET VOICE ROUSED me, but I kicked, fighting to free myself from a tomb of cloth.

"Asher!" The voice raised a few octaves and many decibels as the sheet was yanked from over my head. My sister stood over me, wide-eyed.

"Natalia." My breath was labored and my forehead sweating.

"What's wrong?" Her hair was drenched and glued to her face.

"Why is your hair wet?"

"It isn't." She furrowed her brow.

"Trust me. It is." I looked away. A tendril of morning light seeped around my curtains. "They were open last night."

"What?" Confusion dulled her bright amber eyes.

"The curtains were open last night. Did you close them?"

"No."

"Mother and Father?"

"They're still snoring in their recliners, and their cigarette butts are cold." My sister sat on the bed and wrapped my blanket around her shoulders. Leaning back, she rested her head on a pillow and rolled her lower lip between her teeth.

She touched her hair. "You're right. It is wet."

"It doesn't matter. Just rest," I said. Then I held her hand because her quietness and facial expression told me something was horribly wrong. She wasn't ready to speak, and asking would only cause her to close her mouth more firmly than a crocodile on its prey. Our family's habit—silence.

So I waited, but my heart beat slower because she was there.

"Asher, did you sleep well last night?" She squeezed my hand.

"Not really."

"Why?" Natalia turned and looked at me.

"I heard sounds."

She bolted upright. "So did I."

"When did you hear them?"

She shook her head as if she was shaking free of something. "I don't know." My sister lay back on the pillow, pulling the blanket tighter around her shoulders.

"It was like this." I mimicked the thumping and scraping.

My sister shivered. Her eyes grew wild with fear as she released my hand and walked out of my room.

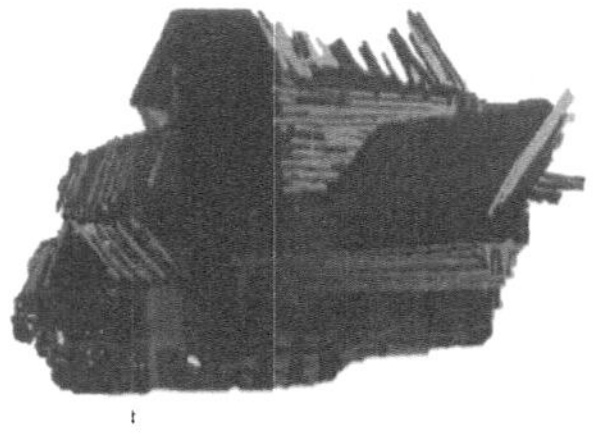

9

A FEW MINUTES LATER, I sat on the edge of my bed, staring at the lake. It wasn't sinister this morning; but strangely, ice caked over the usually placid summer lake. The temperature read seventy degrees on my Galileo thermometer.

I knew I wasn't the bravest boy in my seventh grade class. My classmates had nicknamed me *pollo chiquito*, the little chicken boy, after I refused a dare to hide the teacher's class bell. My classmates were either Jewish kids or WASP kids—nothing in between—so I couldn't understand why they used Spanish to torment me. My sister said that bullies rarely make any sense.

Whatever their reasons, I didn't eat chicken because I hated the name so much. Natalia understood and never served me chicken at lunch or dinner.

"Asher."

"Yes."

"Time for breakfast." I jogged downstairs to the kitchen.

I could sense that Natalia was scared of whatever had happened last night. Knowing she was afraid made my protective instincts kick into gear. Foolishly, I decided to hunt for the source of the sound and end her fear.

How? I didn't know. I'd figure out the details once I started. When I arrived in the kitchen, a raw chicken sat on the kitchen table. Mother donned an apron, handed Natalia a knife, and stood over her. "Cut it just right. I don't want white mixed with dark."

"Yes, Mother."

I rolled my eyes and grabbed a piece of buttered toast. Finally, Mother left the kitchen.

"Are you cooking chicken?" I asked.

"Not for you. I have some casserole tucked away in the back of the refrigerator." Natalia smiled and winked. She was beautiful and thoughtful. "Thanks, sis."

"What are you going to do while I chop this chicken?"

"I'm going out."

"Where?" She laid down the knife.

"Nowhere in particular."

"Don't go to the lake. Do you understand?"

I nodded and left the kitchen. Natalia didn't deserve

to be afraid. I knew I'd better fulfill my mission before I chickened out.

10

SAME MORNING
11:29 A.M.
EAST HAMPTON, NEW YORK

GLANCING OVER MY SHOULDER, I tiptoed through the living room.

No one followed me, so I turned the lock on the west-facing French doors and escaped unnoticed. I tried to devise a plan as I walked the long route around the house. The problem was that I didn't know what I was dealing with.

As I approached the beach, white sand invaded my tennis shoes and chafed my feet. I kept walking until tall seagrass waved and dipped around my legs. I inched closer to the inlet's edge and peered into the sapphire waters. No neon-green eyes. I continued to the other side, heading to the boathouse where the eyes had originated.

The cedar planks of the boathouse were in disrepair. The thought of termites invading wood stirred up an itch in the middle of my scalp, and I scratched as though lice were crawling through my hair.

But then I remembered that termites don't like cedar. The itch subsided, so I stooped low, looking under the edge of the boathouse. No hull rested in the water. The place must be vacant. I proceeded to the front, trudged up the ramp, and pushed on the dilapidated door. It didn't budge. A heavy, rusted chain draped through two handles. An ancient lock held the chains fast.

I sighed, glanced at my house across the inlet, and imagined Natalia's face beaming with pride after I'd slain the monster. I grabbed the chain and tried to shake it loose. The rusty lock loosened, as though invisible hands had unlatched it. The chains clanked to the ground.

My tongue dried. The feeling reminded me of when my mother prescribed punishment for saying a bad word— ten cotton balls stuffed into my mouth. My breath stuck in my throat. I gagged, and then the back of my throat burned. I panted until I finally caught my breath. The creak of metal against metal drove me into another episode of hyperventilation.

Breathe, Asher. Breathe. I inhaled slowly, like my sister did when she practiced breathing techniques for dance.

"Asher, come to me." A strange voice sounding more like a multitude of voices replaced my sister's voice. "Asher, what are you waiting for? Don't you want Annaliese? I can give her to you—then you can have your way with her."

My will to stand firm dissolved.

The doors flung open, hitting the outside walls.

My legs moved me into the boathouse. A cold gust of air chilled my face, and my lips numbed.

My conscience engaged, fighting the mysterious pull. I gripped the edge of the doorjamb. My fingers whitened, then slipped. I toppled onto the floor and rolled to the edge of the wooden planks. My head and shoulders hung over the water. I gripped the edge of the platform.

At first, the water was brown and still. Then it began to churn as though someone had removed a sink stopper. White froth foamed. The grind of metal chains lowering a boat startled me. I jumped to my feet and pressed my back against the stony wall.

"Don't be afraid. I am with you."

I opened my mouth to scream, but I couldn't. The grind of winches and steel cables continued until the hull of a royal-blue boat cracked the ice, splashing frigid slush against the boathouse.

"Annaliese."

Was it my imagination, or did my middle-school crush sit in the back of the boat? Her blonde hair was tied into a ponytail. Her eyelashes fanned up and down, weighted with heavy mascara. Her lips were painted a cherry red. She beckoned me with her forefinger.

"Hi, Asher. I'm here for you."

I walked to the edge of the platform and rested my hand on the boat. Its engine tilted into the water and revved. I stepped back.

"What are you waiting for?" the multitude of voices asked again.

"Who are you?" I looked around the boathouse. A green mist arose behind the boat. Two neon-green dots appeared and then disappeared. A silhouette of a body formed, hovering above the water. The dots were eyes, encircled in red. A row of razor-sharp teeth appeared in the mist. "My name is Nomed, and I've come for a visit."

"You're not welcome here." I gulped back a mouthful of air and a drop of spit.

"Really? Lust told me that you needed a favor."

"Lust?"

"Your lust. Besides, you seem available."

"For what?"

"A houseguest."

"Annaliese lives two houses down. She doesn't need to stay at my house."

"Do you want her or not?"

I looked at her, still in the boat. Her cheeks flushed red, and my knees weakened. "Yes."

"Asher!"

I turned toward the boathouse's open doors, and Natalia stared at me with her hands propped on her narrow waist. "Come back to the house."

I tried to lift my legs, but my feet were as heavy as lead weights. "I can't."

"You must."

"Get her in the boat. She's your sacrifice," Nomed said.

"What do you mean?" I faced the boat again. The mist hovered over Annaliese. She shrunk back in the boat. "Help me, Asher. I need you to protect me."

"But so does Natalia. She's afraid, too," I said.

"Who are you talking to?" Natalia's voice shook.

Thump, scrape, thump, scrape. The invisible pirate was back.

"Asher, the noise from last night!" My sister's eyes became wild and frantic.

"Come to me. I'll protect you." Nomed's mist moved closer to me.

Natalia backed toward the door. "Asher, let's go."

The boathouse door slammed shut, locking us both inside.

"Get her in the boat." The multitude of voices blared in my ear. "She's not safe outside." A sound more deafening than a tornado barreling across the plains pounded in my ears. The weathered windows cracked. I grabbed Natalia's arm, rushing her to the safety of the boat.

"Stop!" Natalia pushed and shoved, then kicked. "Asher, I can't swim."

"Get in the boat. You'll be safe."

"I am safe. What's wrong with you?"

"I just want to protect you from whatever's outside."

Something lifted my sister and slammed her head into a metal post that protruded from the water. Her body went limp.

My heart raced. "Natalia, are you okay?"

She didn't rouse.

"Quick, place her in the boat," Nomed said as the sound grew more deafening.

"You'll keep her safe?" My heart raced faster than my thoughts.

"Isn't Annaliese safe?"

I looked up. Annaliese's face was relaxed. "Yes."

"Trust me."

I dragged my unconscious sister to the boat, then rolled her like a log over the edge. The boat faded into a shadow, losing its solid appearance. My sister's body fell through the mirage, sinking through the opening in the ice. "Natalia!" I threw myself on the plank and reached into the water, grabbing at her hair. A vacuum sucked her down, and she disappeared into the murky brown depths.

I looked back at the boat. "Annaliese?" She'd disappeared.

A laugh emanated from the green mist. The door opened.

"I should have left you in Germany!" a voice said from behind me, scratchier than sandpaper rubbing across wood. I stood up and followed the voice. "Mother?"

"I told your father that you were possessed."

"No!" I couldn't find the words to explain my confused thoughts. "Where's Natalia? She was getting in the boat and then disappeared."

"So that's how it was?" My mother lifted the stub of a cigarette to her mouth and inhaled a long drag. "You're a liar, Asher."

"Mother?"

My mother backed toward the door, never taking her gaze from me. "Your father killed people too. Jews in German ovens—our people."

"What? Father would never do that."

"The apple doesn't fall too far from the tree." She spewed bold words, but her eyes scanned back and forth nervously.

"Asher, I'm here, don't worry." Nomed hovered over me and entered my mouth, filling my body. I felt bigger, taller, larger. Crazily, I wished for a mirror to confirm my new manliness. Mother bolted from the boathouse, across the field, and back toward the house.

"Where's Natalia?" The conversation between the mist and me was no longer audible, but inside my head.

"Exchanged."

"For what?"

"Annaliese."

"I don't want Annaliese anymore. I want my sister."

"Too late. You killed her."

"No . . ." I stuttered. "She fell through the boat."

"The boat was simply a mirage constructed in the recesses of your mind—it gave you the liberty to indulge your pleasures."

I collapsed on the plank and cried. "What did I do wrong?" I looked up toward heaven, angry at the God—Adonai—who had made me short.

"Should've listened to your sister." The multitude of voices taunted me. "Go to Annaliese's house. She's yours. She'll comfort you."

"But I don't want her," I groaned, and then trudged from the boathouse, shoulders down, eyes scanning the ground. I didn't want to leave in case Natalia returned.

Darkness fell.

The air outside was hot, and it warmed my cold skin. She wasn't coming back. I left, passed my house and kept walking toward the house with peach siding—Annaliese's house. Stepping on the porch, I reached up and pressed the doorbell.

Through the front window, I saw a blonde ponytail swishing from side to side as Annaliese skipped to the door.

My face flushed hot.

She opened the door and tilted her head. Her face relaxed. "I'm glad to see you, Asher."

"You are?"

"You look different."

"I do?"

"More . . . powerful. Exciting. Come in."

Those words shot electricity from my brain to my toes. I stepped over her threshold, reached out, and grabbed her hand. "Are your parents here?"

"They're out."

I smiled and followed her to the kitchen. A red plate full of crispy fried chicken sat in the center of the kitchen island. I leaned over the plate and inhaled. It smelled good.

"Want a piece?"

"Sure."

"No longer hating the name *pollo chiquito*?"

"I guess not." I rolled my shoulders back, and Annaliese served me a chicken leg. I bit into it, savoring the flavor. A weight rested on my shoulders. I glanced at Annaliese, then back at my greasy fingers. She pranced over to the kitchen sink and held a glass under the water faucet. I narrowed my eyes, studying her. The weight descended into my body, and something inside me changed my feelings. My desire for her affections ebbed, until only anger burned.

"It's easier the second time." A voice that wasn't my own whispered through my lips.

"No!" I debated within.

"What about Natalia?"

"Leave her alone."

"She's crying. She wants to come back."

"Then give her to me."

"You're demanding, for a murderer."

"I'm not—"

"Quiet—and listen! Do as I say and I'll give her back, awakening you from your dream."

"You mean nightmare?"

"Whatever you say."

II

SUMMER'S ENDED.

Outside, it's cold again.

Six months ago, I had neatly covered Annaliese's corpse under the red blanket on her bed, and, today, the desire to kill again clawed at my will like a vampire begging for human blood. I'd wiped the knife clean, walked into the kitchen, and laid it beside the fried chicken bones. The weight had lifted from my shoulders. My stride was smooth and light as I returned home.

Now, the memory of the killings seemed distant, like fuzzy images in my mind. Natalia hadn't returned. Annaliese's parents had reported their daughter as missing.

This morning, when I entered our house, the radio was off. Mother stared at the black screen that covered the speakers. My father sat in his usual recliner, but his newspaper lay at his feet. I walked between my parents, intending to pass them.

"Asher, we want to speak with you." My father's voice halted, then he cleared his throat. The mute spoke again.

"Yes."

"We're going on a road trip tomorrow morning. Your mother and I've decided. Be ready at 7 a.m. sharp."

"Okay." I climbed the stairs and sat on Natalia's bed. "Natalia, what happened? Why aren't you here?" I leaned over and pressed my hands into my eyes and wept until they were drier than sandpaper.

My thoughts cleared until my mind raced through time and settled near a dilapidated brick building. "Where am I?"

"Manchester, England."

"Why?"

"Look behind you."

A rail-thin boy, his black hair caked with dirt, rummages through a garbage can. A metal trash can tips over on asphalt. A cat hisses a warning. The boy stops, grips his threadbare shirt close, and stares into the distance. The alley remains unoccupied except for the beggar. After lifting a mushy sandwich to his lips, he takes a bite, chews, and finishes his dinner. Black-and-blue prints, the size of a man's hand, cover the boy's face.

"Why would I want to injure a homeless boy? He's smaller than I am!"

"Little boys grow up to be big men who create big problems. Don't be fooled by his helplessness."

"But his face?"

A coarse laugh sounded in my ears. "You're the reason his face looks the way it does."

I stared at my hands. They shook uncontrollably. "What's his name?" My voice broke.

"Joseph."

I sobbed. The presence inside me attempted to comfort me. "Now, there. The boy's a stranger. What about your sister, Natalia? Will you abandon her for a stranger?"

"But I don't want to hurt anyone."

"You already have."

"Joseph's no trouble. I'm sure of it," I beg.

"Rose is."

"Who?"

Joseph's face broke into millions of sand particles. I reached out, trying to rescue the boy. The happy face of a pale-skinned little girl replaced his image and filled my dream. Behind her, children in school uniforms ran across the grassy playground. Their laughter brought back memories of playing chess with Natalia on my parents' front porch.

I cried.

"Here." The pale-faced slight girl hands a piece of bread to another girl who obviously missed her morning face-washing.

"But Rose, your mommy and daddy hardly have any money either."

"My mommy gave me oatmeal, and I'm still full." Rose smiles.

The unwashed girl reaches up and grabs the bread, then devours it. She points. "There's Molly. Are you going to her birthday party this weekend?"

Rose shrugs. "Wasn't invited. Are you going, Emily?"

"Wait a minute." Emily's small meal fuels her legs. She turns her back on Rose and runs toward Molly with a smirk on her face. They talk for a few moments, then prance back to Rose.

Molly places her hands on her hips. "My daddy doesn't like poor people, says they're lazy. You can't come to my party."

Rose backs away, her eyes down. A chain-link fence stops her retreat. She slides down the fence, pulls her knees up, and buries her face in her lap. Between tears, she prays like her daddy told her to. "Yahweh, can you bring my kindred friend before my next birthday?"

I wiped a tear from my eye, coming back from my vision.

"Cry all you want. Trust me, don't let Rose live—or Natalia will be lost forever."

"I can't do it. I won't!"

"You will." Nomed's voice was slow and menacing. "I'll help you."

I backed away from the haunting voice, but Nomed's voice followed me. "Aren't you the forgetful little brother?"

"No." I shook my head. "I love Natalia. You tricked me and made me kill her."

"Tricked is the wrong word. Encouraged—maybe. Give me Joseph and Rose, and then you may have Natalia or Annaliese. Your choice."

"I don't want Annaliese."

"Where is Annaliese?"

"You know where she is," I answered, then pulled back the covers on my sister's empty, cold bed and climbed in. "Why do you care about two kids named Joseph and Rose?"

"They're dangerous."

"My teacher says that Hitler's dangerous, and you don't want him dead."

"Hitler is manageable. They're not, so kill them."

"Then Natalia will return?"

"I promise."

"Where are they?"

"Not born yet."

"Then how could they be dangerous?"

"It all started a long time ago, before your kind invaded our home."

"You're ancient."

"Indeed. It's story time."

"I'm too old for fables, but if your story helps me get Natalia back, go ahead."

"That's my boy. Ezekiel—Elohim's Hebrew prophet— hid a secret scroll in the caves of Makkedah."

"Go find the scroll and leave Natalia and me alone."

"I gave you Annaliese, so finding the scroll is your job."

"You made me kill her."

"That was your choice."

"No, it wasn't. My hand gripped the knife without my

mind's permission. Besides, what do I know about some old scrolls? I wasn't even alive back then."

"But I was, and I am your mind now."

"Why are you bothering me?"

"A host requires preparation."

"Like a chicken's carcass before dinner?"

"I made you popular, didn't I?"

"School isn't even in session. We're on break."

"Annaliese! Remember her? I gave her to you, so be grateful!"

I bolted out of bed, afraid.

"Nothing to fear. I'm your friend." The voice softened, and I felt a cold, clammy hand on my cheek. "I'm your houseguest, and I'm here for a visitation."

My sister was gone. Shoulders rounded, I walked into Natalia's bathroom, flicked on the light, and looked into the mirror. My amber eyes turned neon green. Without my consent, the green eyes flipped behind my eyelids, and my amber eyes reappeared. But I was still short. I lifted my hand, noting the gold ring on my right forefinger. Engraved in the gold was the head of a bull. *How had the ring gotten on my finger?*

Nomed read my thoughts. "I saved it from Nebuchadnezzar's palace."

"Nebuchadnezzar?"

"575 BCE. It's my gift to you. A wedding ring of sorts."

I didn't bother to ask who Nebuchadnezzar was. I assumed I'd be told, whether I wanted the information or not, I sighed.

The next morning, after another hour of driving, a brown sign with white lettering—**SING SING PRISON**—

hung from a horizontal metal pole overhead. My mother stopped at the security gate. My father laid his paper in his lap and leaned toward the driver's window. "Can we take a tour of your old cell block?"

The security guard reentered his office.

"I don't want to," I protested.

My father looked into my eyes. "You'll obey us, or you'll join the murderers."

On the outside, I smiled.

Inside, I cried, remembering Natalia.

Looking into my father's eyes, I recognized his look—deception. They intended to leave me here, so I slid closer to the car door, quietly unlocked it, and planned for my escape. I would silence Reuben and Ruth later. Nomed promised Natalia's return if I killed those children, Joseph and Rose. I would kill them at birth. Why wait? Natalia would come sooner, and we could be happy again. But when would the troublesome pair be born? I opened the door, jumped from the car, and ran.

"It's easier the third time," Nomed said.

"Then why don't *you* murder those children?" My breath was labored as my legs carried me past the chain-link fences.

"I gift you longevity. Obey, and you won't age."

12

TEN YEARS LATER, I STARTED my MBA program at Pennsylvania's Wharton School of Business. During spring break, when the tepid, soft winds were blowing off the Peconic Bay, I returned to my parents' home in East Hampton.

Quietly, I entered Mother's bedroom, gripping the handle of a small knife tucked inside my black leather Balmain jacket. I palmed the weapon. Cold steel warmed my heart. Carefully, I slid the blade out and pressed the flat edge to my thigh. Hand behind my back, I forged ahead to her bed where she lay crying. "It is true, Mother? Am I no longer your son? Am I Leviathan, Job's sea monster?"

"You sound like a . . . Texan."

"Spent a few years in Abilene." I smirk.

"Get out, you monster." My mom stood up from her bed. "Reuuuuben . . ."

With a quickness unnatural for an intellectual with more flab than muscles, I buried the knife deep into Mother's back. Blood spattered. The knife's impact ricocheting off her ribs jarred my shoulder. She screamed and flopped on the bed like a dying fish.

My houseguest spoke. "Finish her off."

I yanked the violin string from my pocket, slid it around her neck, then jerked it upward and back, clinically slicing through her skin, arteries, and trachea.

Mother's body fell, ending her misery and mine.

"You're right, Mother. I am Leviathan." Leaving the front door open, I strolled out of the house, allowing a cool breeze to comb through my hair before I climbed into my lime-green Ford Pinto and headed back to Wharton.

Thoughts bombarded my mind on that long drive. *Firebrands stream from his mouth. Smoke pours from his nostrils as from a boiling pot over a fire of reeds. His breath sets coals ablaze. Strength resides in his neck; dismay goes before him. The folds of his flesh are tightly joined; they are firm and immovable.*

13

I'M FIFTY-ONE YEARS OLD, AND I'm being drawn across the Atlantic Ocean by my houseguest, Nomed, to attend to his business.

My situation has changed.

I no longer drive a Ford Pinto. I'm rich—filthier-than-a-pig rich—and well connected. My company, Sky Media, made me a billionaire media baron.

I stand behind the bow of my Amels superyacht as the captain guides the sleek vessel into a cozy cove off Rathlin Island. I gaze across the Sea of Moyle, admiring the lighthouse on the Mull of Kintyre in Scotland while Abba's track "Dancing Queen" fades into Stevie Wonder's "Isn't She Lovely," reminding me of Natalia. Before the memory siphons the breath from my soul, I suck another drag on my Cuban, allowing the chestnut mixed with cherries to erase any distasteful memories, leaving only the sweet ones of Natalia.

I blow smoke from my nostrils and mouth. The only element missing to transform me into a bona fide dragon is fire spewing from my nostrils. Maybe Nomed can arrange that.

I am Leviathan—Job's sea monster.

Inhaling deeply, I taste salt, the ingredient of the sea and of blood. Since Mother's death, I've not treated my palate to blood, full-bodied liquid that tastes of rusty nails and human fear.

The boy.

The girl.

I lick my lips, yearning for the taste of them.

"Nomed," I whisper into the wind, knowing the fallen one is listening and watching. "In exchange for my dearest Natalia, I offer the pair of troublemakers to you. Do not fail me, Nomed, or I'll be coming for you."

The sky darkens. Beneath the restless sky, Ireland's Antrim Coast unfolds around me, as though an artist is spreading his canvas and telling me to make my own destiny.

Indeed, I will.

Defiant, I stare into a bank of brooding clouds and tell Natalia's God, "You stay up there, and I'll stay down here. Deal?"

A jagged lightning bolt arcs across the sky. And just like when I'd tried to decipher my father's grunts, I don't know if Natalia's God is answering my demands with a yes or no.

As I wait for another boat, I sense a curious tune rising in me. *If I could be a minnow, minnow, minnow. If I could be a minnow, I'd swim out to the deep blue sea.*

Finishing the mournful melody, I remove the fat cigar from my lips, kiss the palm of my hand, and blow the kiss into the fierce winds. "To Natalia, my precious, perfect, righteous sister . . . gone too soon."

—The End—

Dear Reader,

"HouseGuest" is different from the rest of the Orphan Dreamer Saga and could be categorized as a paranormal short story with hints of horror. It is best read after *Orphan Dreamer and the Glass Tattoo*, the first novel in the *Orphan Dreamer* series. The themes in "HouseGuest" were difficult to depict in my normal writing style, but the rest of the stories in the series are all written as suspenseful mysteries.

If you enjoyed "HouseGuest," please take a moment to post a review wherever you purchased this novelette, sharing with other readers what you've learned and liked. If you didn't like the short story, please send me your opinions via the Contact Us page on my website: www.JNellBrown.com. Your feedback is invaluable.

The A21 Campaign, a nonprofit organization that works to abolish the human-trafficking of children, receives a percentage of the proceeds from all of my novels.

Thank you for reading this story. I look forward to meeting you on Facebook. Please like my page so you can follow my writing journey. Also, please sign up for my newsletter, and I will notify you about future releases, sales and special events.

With gratitude,
J. Nell Brown

Acknowledgments

Yeshua, thank you for inspiring this book through my imagination at a time when I needed it most. You've always been faithful to me.

Special thanks to my late father, Chaplain Austin Brown; my mother, Mrs. Jeanette Brown; and my sisters and friends.

To my editors, Ann Castro and Emily Dings at AnnCastro Studio, Faralee Pozo at Upwork.com, and Courtney Rae Andersson at Elevation Editorial—thank you all for your eagle-eye talents.

To my readers, thank you for loving this story. These characters exist for you.

Author Biography

J. Nell Brown, the daughter of a chaplain and a teacher, is a Florida native.

Her relationship with Yeshua (Jesus) is fused with experiences in life, travel, extensive Bible study, and people's stories, and she combines all of this to create characters, plots, and settings for her novels and short stories. An involuntary insomniac, Brown practices medicine and writes in her free time.

She is a self-proclaimed nerd and loves all things scientific. Her love of science is demonstrated by her research at Los Alamos National Laboratory, the site for the development of the atomic bomb. She graduated with honors from the University of Florida (U of F) College of Agriculture and received her medical doctorate from the same. After completing an anesthesia residency at The University of Chicago Hospitals, she practices in Florida.

Her heart overflows with compassion for hurting people, particularly children. A portion of the proceeds from this book will go to the A21 Campaign, a rescue charity for human-trafficked children, and Eastside Baptist School in Gainesville, Florida, a school of love, values, and solid educational curriculum for children whose parents would not otherwise be able to afford an alternative school education.

Her first nonfiction book, *Shhh, My Father Is Speaking, and I Am Listening*, is about her prayer journey. The Bible is her favorite literary masterpiece. You may follow J. Nell Brown on her author website, JNellBrown.com.

A Generation of Lighted Evergreens

1—Sugarcane

12:00 P.M.
FRIDAY, AUGUST 11, 1967
BELLE GLADE, FLORIDA

AUSTIN CAVANAUGH HAD BEEN IN the same position for the last five hours—slightly hunched with a machete in his right hand, chopping sugarcane in a hot, humid field.

He laid the cutlass by his feet, dug in his pocket, and retrieved a gray-brown handkerchief, a Christmas gift from his father, who had been a peanut farmer. Dabbing his forehead, he soaked up droplets of sweat, a field hand's reminder that the old fireball didn't play favorites. "Whaddya say, 'bout time for some water, Chuck?"

"When the boss man says so." Chuck kept chopping

down stalks of cane. He was Austin's local friend and had grown up in Gainesville, Florida, down the dirt road from Austin's father's peanut farm.

"Ain't no rest for the weary . . ." Austin's arm ached as he gripped the wooden handle of his machete, swiping the blade through another clump of thick cane.

"You ain't takin' a break without the whistle chirpin', are ya?" Riddled with the remnants of untreated pneumonia and asthma, Chuck hacked up strands of mustard-colored phlegm. The dirt and pollen hadn't helped his allergies or lung infection.

"Nope—just dreamin'."

"What about?"

"A cozy place in the country, a vegetable garden, a few chickens, a hammock, and a tall glass of ice-cold lemonade." Austin kneaded his wrist, easing the constant throb. "How's the pneumonia?"

"I ain't laid out yet. You'll know it's bad when I fall over dead."

"Don't want it to come to that. Will the doc see you?"

"He ain't never seen no colored people."

"But he takes care of sick people, don't he?"

"Yep."

"You're sick."

"You done died and gone to heaven. Yes, sirree." Chuck rocked back on his heels, his thumbs tucked beneath his blue suspenders. "You lost your mind somewhere in this cane field." As though stepping on a drumline, Chuck dipped to the right. "Go on wit yo bad self."

Austin gazed into the heavens. Closing his eyes, he allowed Florida's sun to bake his skin to a deeper brown.

No need to keep the sun from doing her business. Brown was brown in the South. It didn't matter if you had one teaspoon of cream in your DNA or ten, so be proud of the Almighty's doing.

"Whatcha doin'?"

"Thinkin'."

"Oh, Lord . . ." Chuck's gaze skimmed over the cane field.

A channel of wind found its way between the stalks. Leaves slipped by each other, creating a fan.

Opening his eyes, Austin turned and stared down the wide dirt road that wound like a diamondback rattlesnake. The dirt and pebble path ended at the big house—a white, rectangular clapboard building adorned with black shutters and six twelve-pane windows. A deep wraparound porch encircled the boss's field house like his belt—low and dipping in the front. Austin knew about the belt because the boss had chased him down the road, threatening to use it.

The reason?

Austin's yellow lab, Gus, hadn't stayed put—the boss had found him down the main road, tucked beneath a shrub. Old Gus had probably spotted the shady boughs of the sugarcane field's lone oak tree and decided he needed a little more cool air, or he had mindlessly chased a squirrel, which gave him an excuse to track his master's scent. The reason hadn't mattered, and since then, Austin had shut Gus inside their wooden shack by the stream.

Hope he's not gone and fainted in that old shed. Couldn't bear to find him laid out from the heat.

Hunching low, Chuck tiptoed to Austin's side, breaking his thoughts. When Chuck grinned, a space the size of a man's thumb separated his dingy teeth—teeth like a black-top wedged between two dirty-white fishtail Cadillacs. A drunken brawl in the juke joint had claimed his missing teeth, but who was Austin to judge a man's past? He swept his machete across the bases of several stalks of cane, excising them with an executioner's accuracy.

One paycheck closer to a better life.

Orphan Dreamer and the Glass Tattoo

39—Adelaide: #Goodbye. Mom and Dad

The Present. The End . . .
03:49 A.M.
Friday. May 11
Exeter. New Hampshire

I SHOULD BE SLEEPING.

I want to, but I can't.

Rain falls, thrumming down the windowpanes of my dorm, smearing a haze across the night sky. I tug my great-great-grandmother's quilt up over my slight frame, blocking the night winds as they slap dead branches against the windows before seeping around rotting-wood casements and swirling around the room.

Cordy's asleep.

I'm jealous.

A ghoulish hand seems to slide through the night, clutching a sickle in its bloodless grasp. Its icy presence chills me to my bones.

Desperate to shake the creepy feeling I've had all day, I borrowed Gage's prayer candles. I light them. They flicker, casting shadows on bare walls but refusing to give me any comfort as they burn inside small red votives, leaving pools of wax in glass. Why do people burn candles in religious ceremonies anyway? I tighten my grip around Mother's letter. *My Dearest Adelaide Rose . . .*

She adored the Seurat painting, and now it belongs to me.

Where would I hang it? The dorms? Priceless paintings combined with chipped, pressboard furniture? Definitely bad Feng Shui.

Where would I live after Mother died?

The day before Da disappeared, he'd called me at 5:00 a.m. EST and confessed why he was acting weird—spontaneous.

"Yer mother's dying, lass. I dinna know how else to say it to you."

"Can we help her?" I asked.

"I canna save her. Her doctor says it's too late for a lung transplant." My da's voice sounded as though it would break, not a frequent occurrence. His physical presence usually barked, "Think twice before acting stupid."

"What is she dying from?"

"Blood's floodin' her lungs, and she's drownin'. Fate's cruel. She's always hated water—lakes, oceans, pools—it didna matter. Never mastered swimmin'. Now her heart's broken, and I'm tellin' the good Lord, I didna break it. I'm a man of blood. I've never deserved her."

I'm a man of blood. I never deserved her.

My heart skips a beat, then pounds my ribs.

I tuck Mother's note inside my flannel pajamas, placing it close to my heart as I thought about Da's phone call. "Mummy, get better. Stay a while longer, please?" I breathe the plea into the darkness, but my voice won't travel the hundreds of miles from New Hampshire to the Blue Ridge Mountains of North Carolina where she lives alone with Beatha, her friend and, according to Father, her nurse.

It sucks to be a teenager.

Adults keep us in the dark and then wonder why we bump into things.

I need clarity. I've never done this before—closed my eyes, knelt, and prayed. "A month longer with Mummy. That's all I ask. Let her watch me graduate."

I open my eyes, already knowing that today is going to be a sucky, armpit kind of day. Since leaving the library and going to bed, I've been staring at the ceiling for six hours.

Red block numbers on the face of my digital clock tell me it is 3:49 in the morning.

Before the sun dares to rise, I slip on a pair of spandex leggings, a lavender hoodie, well-worn trainers, and my shoulder lamp, then stuff my mother's letter into the hoodie pocket. I need to be near her. The letter is all I have.

Tiptoeing from my dorm room, I'm careful to not wake Cordelia.

I need to be alone.

Beneath an audience of stars, I jog across the slick, wet grounds of Exeter Academy. Cold sweat drips down my back. Endorphins flood my muscles, and I pump my arms and legs harder, charging past my lecture hall, a redbrick, four-story building hidden behind a cluster of maple trees. Fog hovers over the lawn, and crickets whistle a nightingale's song.

Out of nowhere, a wobbly form charges toward me.

My heart races, fueling my legs.

The creature's stride quickens, and as it comes closer, I recognize him. He's uglier in the dark, like a swamp monster on two legs.